Rattletrack Road

Written by John Parsons

Illustrated by Betty Greenhatch

Contents

Meet the Characters

Juniper

A clever student.

Mrs Humphries

A rattled driver who is Juniper and Theo's mum.

Theo

Juniper's little brother.

Mr Humphries

Another rattled driver who is Juniper and Theo's dad.

Mr Bonito

A neighbour.

Dear Reader

The town I used to live in had the bumpiest roads you could imagine. It was almost like driving on a safari, except there weren't quite as many lions or giraffes. One day, I was thudding and juddering my way to the post office when I thought, "Some people would find this fun!" And thoughts like that are how stories start!

John Parsons

Author

Pinecone Valley

1. The freeway
2. Rattletrack Road

1 Puddles and Potholes

THUMP! CRASH! Holding a carton of eggs, Juniper Humphries fell across the back seat. She bounced against her brother Theo. In the front seat, Juniper's mum grimly held the steering wheel.

The wipers flicked thick blobs of mud off the windscreen.

"Oh no!" said Mrs Humphries, who had just been to the salon. "My hairdo is ruined!"

There was another thump, and another splash of mud. Like a jack-in-the-box, Mrs Humphries' hairdo hit the car roof again.

"Mum!" complained Theo. "Juniper sat on my video game!"

EGGS

"I'm trying to save these eggs," said Juniper.

JUDDER! JUDDER! JUDDER!

The car made a sound like a washing machine.

Mrs Humphries steered through the last of the puddles and potholes on Rattletrack Road. With a sigh of relief, she drove onto the main street of Pinecone Valley.

"Someone really should do something about that road," she complained. "It's the only road into Pinecone Valley from the freeway. It's ten kilometres of pure disgrace."

"Someone should do something about big sisters who sit on video games!" added Theo.

He pushed his sister. Juniper yelped – and dropped the carton of eggs.

"Now look what you made me do!" she complained. "They were fine on Rattletrack Road – and now look at them!"

Soon, they were home. Mrs Humphries, Theo, and Juniper all climbed out, and slammed the car doors.

"Hello!" called Mr Humphries from the driveway. "My, that's a nice hairdo," he smiled.

Mrs Humphries let out a sound like a grumpy lion that has just had its tail pulled. Mr Humphries suddenly remembered an urgent job to do in the garage – the neighbour's garage.

2 What Will We Do?

"It is a problem," agreed Mr Bonito, the neighbour. "We really do need more visitors to our town, or the few shops we have left will close. Then what will we do?"

Mr Humphries was sitting on a tool box in Mr Bonito's garage.

"Pinecone Valley could be a great tourist spot," he said. "We have great scenery and great people. But folks just want to drive on smooth freeways." He shrugged. "They need a reason to turn off."

"We've tried market days," said Mr Bonito. "No one came."

"Then we tried a band in the main street," said Mr Humphries. "No one turned up."

"We tried dressing in old-fashioned costumes," sighed Mr Bonito. "Still no tourists."

"No one wants to drive over Rattletrack Road to get here," said Mr Humphries. "What will we do?"

Mr Bonito winked. "We're holding a contest for ideas," he said. "Maybe ..."

There was a knock on the garage door. It was Mrs Humphries.

"Sorry," she said, smiling at Mr Humphries. "I didn't mean to be a grump."

"Hello, Mrs Humphries," said Mr Bonito. "That is a nice hairdo!"

On Monday afternoon, Juniper Humphries walked home from Pinecone Valley School. She saw a sign on the window of Mr Bonito's stationery shop.

"Contest!" it said. "You are invited to submit ideas to increase the number of tourists coming to our town. All welcome. $100 for the best idea!"

A hundred dollars!

Juniper wondered if that would be enough to buy a new brother. She was sure the one she had was past his use-by date. She went home, thinking about the contest.

She was doing a project on advertising at school. She had a few ideas.

3 An Idea

At the town meeting, no one put their hand up when Mr Bonito called for new ideas.

"Let's face it," said Mrs Delaware, the bakery owner. "No one will come to Pinecone Valley while our road is so bad."

"It doesn't matter how good our ideas are," said Mr Samuels, the butcher. "When people hit Rattletrack Road, they usually turn around and go back to the freeway."

"I have an idea," came a voice from the back of the room. Mr Bonito peered over the people.

"Why, it's Juniper Humphries. What's your idea, young lady?"

Juniper told everyone her idea. The group listened. And listened. And soon, even Mrs Delaware and Mr Samuels were nodding.

"It's worth a try," said Mr Bonito.

Later that week, everyone in Pinecone Valley held another meeting at the school.

"Let's list the worst things about our terrible Rattletrack Road," said Juniper. She stood in front of the board.

"It's the worst ten kilometres you could ever drive over," said her dad.

"It has puddles that could drown an army tank!" called Mrs Delaware.

"It has potholes bigger than the Grand Canyon!" added Mr Samuels.

"It has more mud than a hippo would know what to do with," said Mr Bonito.

"You have to be as tough as a big-time wrestler to hold a steering wheel the whole way," said Juniper's mum.

As TOUGH AS A big-time WRESTLER ...

More MUD *than* A HIPPO know what *to do* with

Soon Juniper had a list that filled half of the board.

"Now," she said. "Next comes the advertising magic!"

Everyone leaned forward as Juniper got to work.

4 A New Tourist Attraction

The next month was busy – very busy indeed!

There were signs to build. There were brochures to write. There were newspapers to phone. Everyone was busy promoting Pinecone Valley's newest attraction.

Then, one spring day, Rattletrack Road was at its bumpiest, rattliest, puddliest worst. Everyone drove out to the freeway. The new sign for Pinecone Valley was ready – and the

local paper wanted everyone to be in a photo for the front page.

Everyone lined up in front of their muddy cars and trucks, beneath the new sign.

"OK, if everyone is ready, let's all smile!" called out the photographer.

"I hope this works," whispered Mr Bonito.

"I hope we don't look silly," said Mrs Delaware. "Is my hair OK?"

"We're counting on you, young lady," said Mr Samuels.

"Don't worry," grinned Juniper. "No one can resist a really good sign."

“OK!” called out the photographer. “Let’s see the sign!”

Juniper tugged on the rope that held a sheet over the sign.

The camera clicked, and everyone stared up at the sign.

Then everyone clapped. Pinecone Valley’s newest tourist attraction was now open!

5 A Real Tourist Spot

It was the last Sunday in the month.

There wasn't one car park left in the main street of Pinecone Valley. Mr Samuels was at a barbecue stall, selling sausages and hot dogs as fast as he could. Mrs Delaware was putting fresh cakes and buns in her bakery window. A queue of happy people lined up outside Mr Bonito's stationery store.

People were taking photos of each other in front of their muddy cars, looking very proud.

"I've never seen so many people in Pinecone Valley," said Mrs Humphries.

"We're a real tourist spot now," agreed Mr Humphries.

"Hey, where's Juniper?" asked Theo, looking up from his video game.

"She's inside Mr Bonito's store, signing certificates," said Mrs Humphries. "After all, your sister is now a star."

Mrs Humphries pointed to the news cutting inside Mr Bonito's shop window.

Above the article was a photo. Juniper was standing beneath the new sign that read:

"ARE YOU TOUGH ENOUGH TO VISIT PINECONE VALLEY?"

A picture of a famous big-time wrestler looked down.

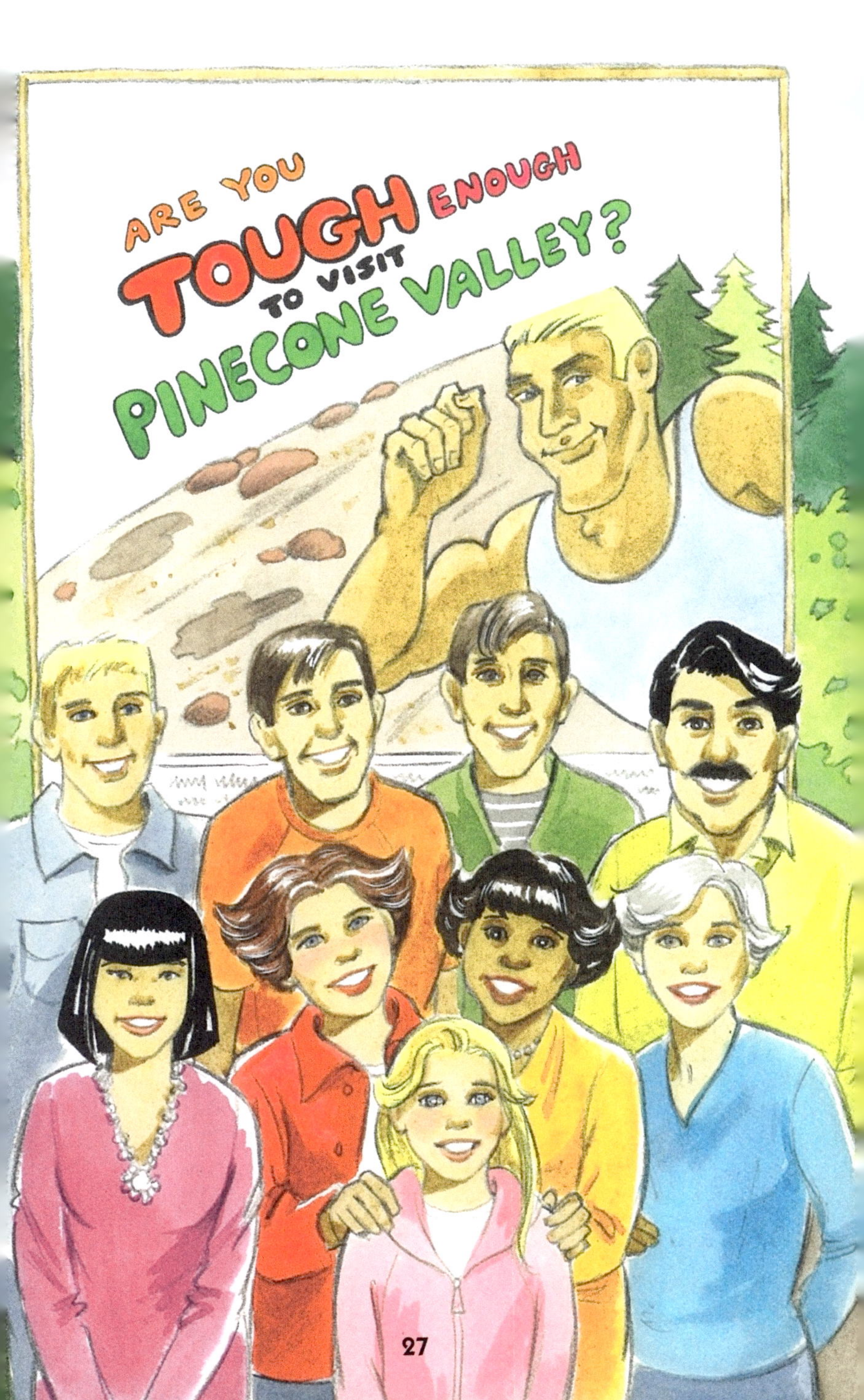
ARE YOU
TOUGH ENOUGH
TO VISIT
PINECONE VALLEY?

The rest of the sign read:

"Are **you** ready for the worst ten kilometres you could ever drive?
Tackle puddles that could **drown an army tank**!
Attack potholes bigger than the **Grand Canyon**!
Wallow in mud that would **hide a hippo**!

"THERE'S ONLY ONE WAY TO GET THE EXCLUSIVE RATTLETRACK ROAD SURVIVOR'S CERTIFICATE – **AND IT'S THIS WAY!**"

With one good idea, Juniper and the townspeople had changed Rattletrack Road. It was no longer the reason no one visited. A few clever words had turned it into the reason *everyone* visited.

None of the visitors could resist a challenge – and everyone wanted to have something exclusive.

As Juniper had realised, you just need to turn the negatives into positives.